ONE LITTLE
CHICKADEE

One
Little
Chickadee

by **MARILEE ROBIN BURTON**
pictures by **JANET STREET**

Tambourine Books
New York

Library of Congress Cataloging in Publication Data

Burton, Marilee Robin. One little chickadee/by Marilee Robin Burton; illustrated by Janet Street. —
1st ed. p. cm. Summary: A counting book with groups of animals from one to ten making
various kinds of noises. [1.Animal sounds—Fiction. 2. Counting. 3. Stories in rhyme.]
I. Street, Janet, ill. II. Title. PZ8.3.B969On 1994 [E]—dc20 93-27271 CIP AC
ISBN 0-688-12651-0 (trade). — ISBN 0-688-12652-9 (lib. bdg.)
10 9 8 7 6 5 4 3 2 1
First edition

To Uncle Artie   M.R.B.

For Golda   J.S.

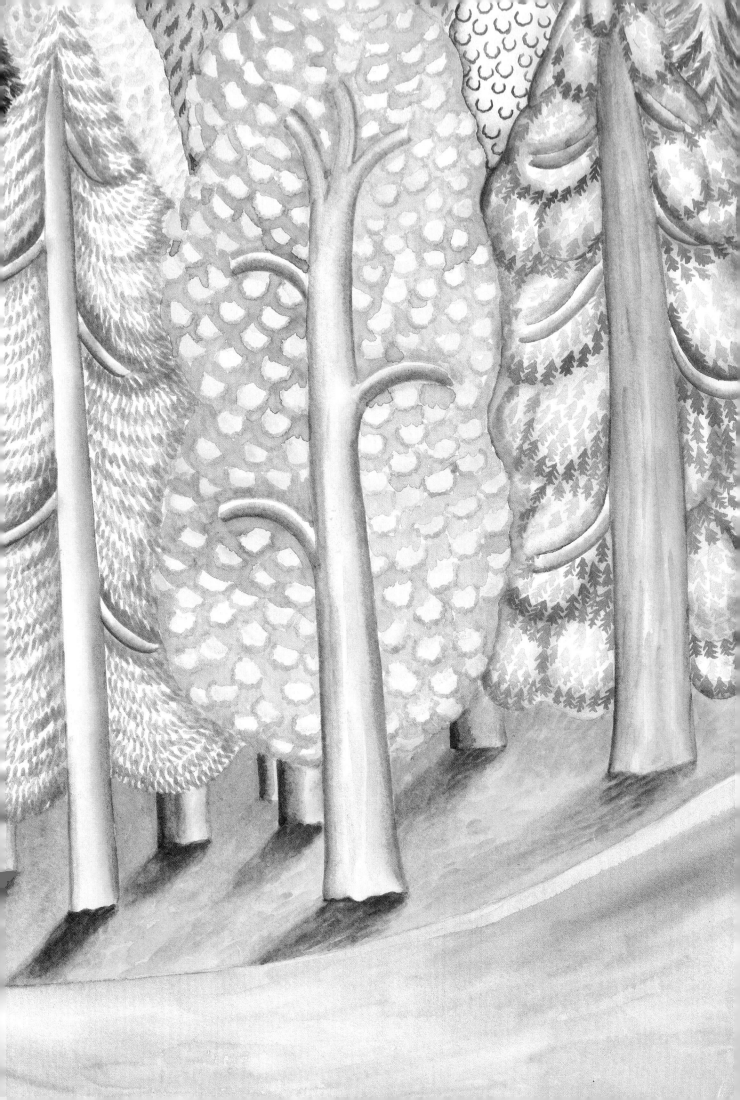

One little chickadee flew to a tree.
He was as lonely as lonely could be.
He stood and he stood and he stood and he stood,
One little bird all alone in a wood.

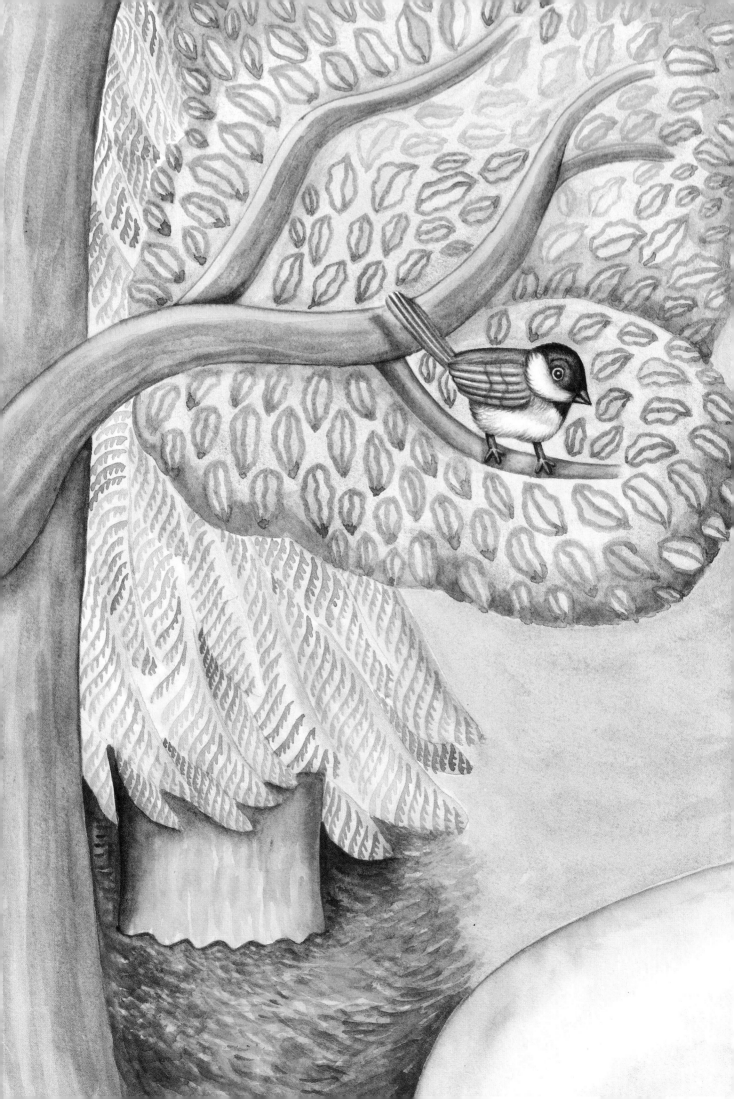

Two small starlings came and sat below.
One looked up and said, "Hello."
Before very long they were up in the tree
Twittering, tweeting, and trilling, all three.

Three young cockatoos joined in the troupe.
Together they made quite a clamorous group.
They whistled and warbled and chanted and sang.
All through the forest their birdsong rang.

ST. JOHN'S LIBRARY

Four curious kittens heard the song
And quietly listened, but not for long.
Soon they scampered way up high
And mewed their meows into the sky.

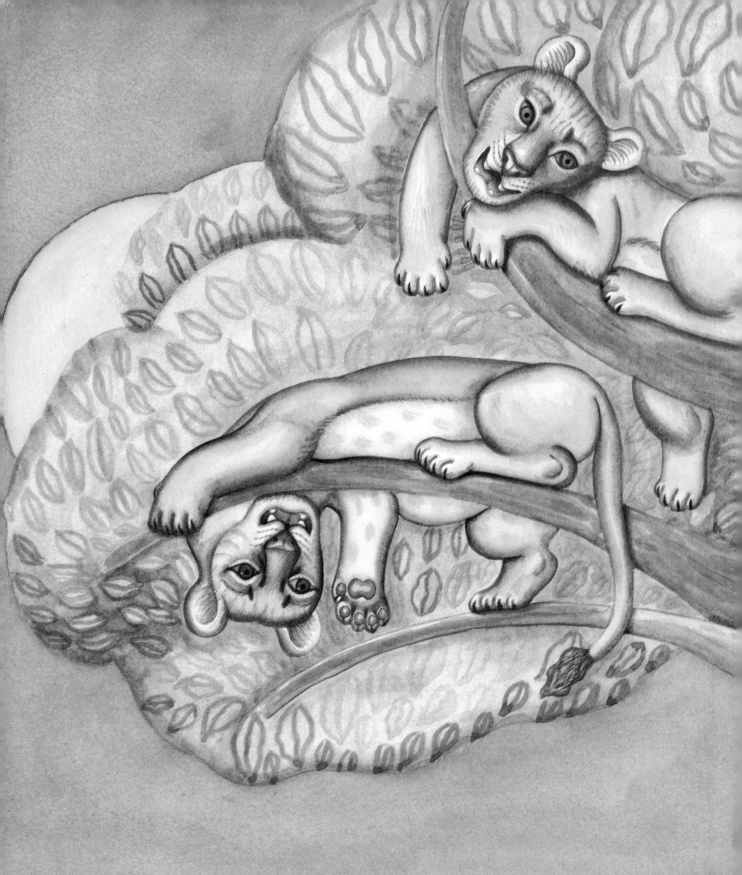

Five frisky lion cubs rambling free
Decided to join in the jamboree,
Climbing way up to the very top,
Roaring and roaring, not wanting to stop.

Six trotting ponies who gamboled nearby
Heard that grand melody high up in the sky.
So they pranced to the tree and began to neigh,
Singing, "neigh neigh neigh" all the rest of the day.

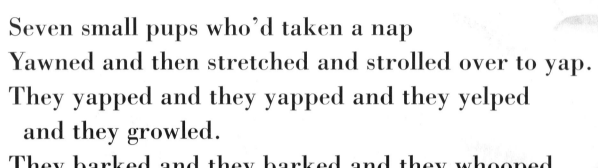

Seven small pups who'd taken a nap
Yawned and then stretched and strolled over to yap.
They yapped and they yapped and they yelped
 and they growled.
They barked and they barked and they whooped
 and they howled.

Eight little hippos down on the ground
Heard all the music and danced around.
They looked and they listened, they romped
  and they stomped.
They listened some more, then they clomped.

Nine chatty monkeys out for a walk
Stopped at the tree and started to talk,
Chittering and chattering to everyone there.
It mattered not who. They did not care.

Ten small bears in a neighboring tree
Scrambled on over to look and to see.
They sat in each branch and looked at the crowd,
Then rumbled and grumbled remarkably loud.

ST._JOHN'S LIBRARY

A vexed crowd of moms heard all the rattle
And came running over fearing a battle.
Finding their babes, each one with a grin,
They gathered them up, took them home,
  tucked them in.

Now one little chickadee so snug in his nest
Laughed as he dreamed, contented to rest.
He was as happy as happy could be,
One little bird in his bed, in his tree.